AF206915

Heinz Landon-Burgher

RSD

Travel Service

0800-503 575 890

A crime story

Produced and published by:
BoD – Books on Demand, Norderstedt
Copyright: 2019 Karl Heinz Landenberger
ISBN 978-3-7460-0719-9

Preface:

This is a true story. The events described really happened. The telephone numbers and bank accounts exist in real life. Even the names of the people involved in this story have not been changed. The goal is to make thousands of people aware that they may have unknowingly fallen victim to a scam. I myself did not realize that I had been scammed until five years later.

Holidays in Turkey

Turkey is a beautiful holiday destination. It offers glorious beaches, the warm sea water, spacious, modern hotel facilities, good – yes, very good – food and the uniquely affordable prices. I have visited the country at least eight times with all kinds of travel companies as well as on my own.

Study Trips

I also went on a study trip twice with RSD Travel Service. One was a trip to Cappadocia and the other a tour around the northern, Turkish part of the island of Cyprus. Both trips left nothing to be desired, with the holiday in Turkey meeting all expectations as usual.

RSD Travel Service

This travel agency lists Eisenheimerstraße 61, Munich 80687 as its address. It is a limited liability company. By phone, the company can be reached at 0800-505 243 097, where you can book the trip you are looking for. It encloses its brochures in renowned publications such as medical journals or directs them at home and property owners. Or to put it more plainly, with readers from the wealthier section of the population.

Unique, Affordable Prices

There is a saying that goes "Among the rich, you learn to save". In line with this motto, RSD offered their trips at unbeatably low prices. The most recent offer is a sensational, exclusive study trip to Morocco followed by another week of relaxing in Marrakech in a 4-star hotel of your dreams. And all that at the preferential price of €199.00 instead of €1,199.00, therefore €1,000.00 cheaper.

Expanded Program

I myself have gone on a Morocco trip with this company in the past and was fully satisfied. I have even traveled as far as the United Arab Emirates with RSD Travel Service. They are constantly expanding their program. The flights depart from eight German airports, thus from all major cities.

Off-season

One special feature is that all travel dates are in the off-season. The dates are therefore only noticed by people that don't have any children at school, that is, pensioners or singles. Turkey's hotels, filled to overflowing during peak season, are empty at that time, which explains the unusually low price.

Government Subsidy?

The Turkish state allegedly pays every traveler during this time a certain subsidy, as doing so is far cheaper than paying out unemployment benefits to all the newly unemployed hotel employees. It is a convenient regulation for all those involved.

Purchases

The travelers also spend quite a bit of money: special excursions and special entry prices, for example, have to be paid for separately. Given that only the overnight stay and breakfast are included in the package, lunch and dinner also have to be paid for every day. That goes without saying.

Final Day

But the last day arrives on every trip. On this day, the travelers are driven to a large leather shop, a jewelry center and a carpet center. The well-to-do retirees and pensioners regularly spend good money there.

Me Too

After the Cappadocia trip, we were driven to a carpet factory. It was extremely interesting. There, we were able to see how the carpet knotters knotted their double knots while working, and the different patterns they used. I found how the silk threads were made from the cocoon of the silkworm fascinating. Despite the fact that I didn't have any more room for yet another hand-knotted rug in my apartment, I couldn't resist buying at least a small one. This now lies in the hallway over my Afghan. It was not too expensive, a wool carpet with no silk, and the knotting was not overly fine, but it had bold colors and a pattern to match.

Jewelry Center

We then went to a jewelry center, apparently the largest of its kind in Turkey. It was very grand and we were told that the prices had been set by the state. Haggling was therefore not an option.

The building is huge and modern. The ground floor houses the goldsmithing workshops, and whenever you walk in, you can see a good dozen of goldsmiths behind their workbenches through the glass windows. They file and sand and fit gemstones into premade frames for rings, brooches and necklaces. It is extremely impressive, and straight away it is clear to see that Turkey is among the world's best when it comes to jewels.

Girlfriend

I had actually intended to come on this trip with my long-term girlfriend. Everything had already been paid for. The extra costs for excursions, full board, departure dates, and so on. However, three days before the trip, she fell ill and had to be admitted to hospital. Given that her condition was not, too worrying, however, and I hadn't taken out cancelation insurance, I dared to set off on the journey alone.

Souvenirs

She came from a jeweler's family and really appreciates beautiful jewelry. So, I decided that I would take at least one beautiful ring home for her. Her favorite stones are sapphire, ruby and emerald. These gems are displayed in overwhelming abundance on the upper floor of the center. I quickly discovered a gorgeous ruby ring adorned with large rubies and many small diamonds. A beautiful sapphire surrounded by diamonds also caught my eye. There was a second sapphire next to it, and I just couldn't decide between the two. In the end, I didn't want to leave without an emerald either. So, on a complete whim, I bought four rings.

Customs

But now there was a big problem. This purchase far exceeded the upper limit for goods that could be taken home without paying customs. However, I didn't want to risk smuggling them back. The center found a solution. They apparently had an agreement with customs that allowed them to ship the rings to me without customs charges. They could register the jewelry as paid at customs for a lower price. But I would not be allowed to have any paid receipts or certificates in my possession during luggage checks at customs. I therefore had to trust that my rings would actually be delivered to me.

Trust

Given that it was such a huge center with an estimated 200 sellers and employees, I was so trusting that I left without any receipt for my payment, giving them merely my home address.

A Feudal Lunch

For this reason, however, it took longer to process my transaction. By this time, my group was already at the exit and ready to board the bus to drive to lunch. My seller offered to take me out to a refined restaurant for lunch. Afterwards, a chauffeur would bring me back from there to my group, who were already in a shop dealing in fine leather goods. It was a very noble gesture by the jewelry center. They had chosen a fine restaurant with exquisite and expensive dishes that I had never had before.

Delivery

Two to three weeks later already, when I was back home, the parcel arrived from D Jewels. On the color-printed envelopes depicting my rings, there were handwritten notes on how many carats the gems, smaller diamonds and the gold consisted of. The name of the seller was also printed there. The parcel also came with an assurance that the jewelry pieces could be exchanged for other goods of the same value within five years.

Inconvenience

There was one small inconvenience, however, that wouldn't go away. RSD Travel Service had sent a letter prompting me to pay the single occupancy price for the room as I had embarked on the trip alone. I was speechless. I had already paid for the full trip as well as all surcharges for two people and now I was being expected to pay a single occupancy surcharge just because my partner had been ill.

Single Occupancy Surcharge

I couldn't accept that. But RSD was going so far as to threaten with a lawsuit. Several letters were exchanged back and forth. It was only when I had made it clear that I was willing to come to court proceedings that RSD backed down.

After that, however, RSD drastically increased their single occupancy surcharges. The latest study trips to Morocco for autumn 2019 and spring 2020 cost €199.00 per person, but the single occupancy surcharge is €299.00 per person. This makes it clear that the trip could only be financed through surcharges. Actually, it's also clear that no one can offer 14 days in Morocco with flights, a round tour and a week of relaxation in a 4-star hotel for just €199.00. Just where is the money coming from?

Northern Cyprus

The following year on my trip to Northern Cyprus, I had to travel alone from the outset. At that point, my girlfriend had become seriously ill. Normally, solo travelers are rejected despite the increased single occupancy surcharge, but I had a promotional code. This obviously kept an account of who the buyer was and I was able to go on the trip without any issues.

Travel Guide

The travel guide for this fascinating trip to the northern part of the island – I had already been to the south – was incredibly likeable. He had been born in Germany, in the Ruhr district and spoke German with no trace of an accent. But when he was 20, he was convinced that he would find more professional opportunities in Turkey than in Germany and decided to return to his parents' homeland. Thanks to his excellent German skills, he became one of the most popular travel guides there. RSD Travel Service has meanwhile reached 65,000 air passengers a year, an economic factor that should be taken seriously. Most of these guests fly to Turkey.

Antalya

This trip, too, ended in Antalya and of course, in the gigantic jewelry center D Jewels, where I had shopped beyond my means just one year previously. I was determined not to buy anything this time, considering that the four rings had not gone down too well with my girlfriend. She had a very particular taste and had told me plainly that she didn't like a single one of the four rings.

Solitaire

Two young women, friends that had already taken this trip together before, were sitting in the same row with me on the bus. We had already talked and laughed a lot together. I confessed my weakness for beautiful jewels to them and asked for their support to stop me from making the mistake of going over my budget again. We bravely walked past all the jewels until a solitaire with a large, shining diamond caught my eye. Under no circumstances did I want to buy it. I was simply interested in how much a gem like that cost. Next to every large display case, there is a small office where a customer advisor provides information about the jewelry pieces displayed. All I wanted was to know the price. The two women called after me, "Don't forget, you don't want to buy it!" But it was no use. The disaster took its course.

A Turkish Woman from Reutlingen

When the nice young Turkish woman noticed that I liked the diamond ring, she couldn't be stopped. There was something very attractive about her Swabian-Turkish accent. She had lived in Reutlingen for many years and... and... and... what she most missed in Turkey were those good Swabian pretzels. Next time, I would have to be sure to bring her one.

Price

So, how much did this solitaire cost? She didn't want to cough up the price straight away.
"We have very beautiful diamonds, so much cheaper. Do you not want to at least take a look at these?" No, actually! I only wanted to know the price of this particular diamond.
"Well, it is very expensive. A unique sample, when it comes to clarity and cut. It costs €72,000.00."
Wow! I was stunned. That was well beyond my means. What's more, I didn't want to buy it just for the sake of it. I thanked her for the information and turned to leave.

Dr. Kaya

But things weren't quite that simple.
"Wait, wait! Today is a very special day. The owner of the jewelry center himself is here today as an exception. He can grant you conditions that we aren't allowed to."
There were no conditions that could convince me to buy such an expensive diamond. But Dr. Kaya was already standing in the doorway and introduced himself.

Don't Buy It!

He told me about his company and its many branches. I couldn't get away without appearing impolite. He had run after me and overheard us without us noticing. He had apparently been very annoyed to hear the two women call "Don't buy it!" after me. I thought his remark rather inappropriate.

An Armenian

But then he told such an interesting story about himself that I couldn't help but listen, intrigued. He was Armenian, but now mainly lived in Istanbul. Armenians are still not very popular in Turkey, which is why he had a Turkish name there. He wasn't wearing a name tag, but it probably would have displayed his Turkish name. He had taken it off beforehand, but worried that I may have been able to read it and felt the need to explain why he was now introducing himself under his Armenian name Dr. Kaya. He still owned land in the original Armenian homeland, near Lake Van in East Anatolia, where the Armenian resistance against the Sultan had taken place at the beginning of the First World War and from where the string of refugees had then moved toward the desert area north of Syria.

String of Refugees

Of this string of refugees, forced out by the Turkish military, only a few arrived in Musa Dagh. Most of them had died of exhaustion or starvation or had fallen victim to massacres that took place in Turkish villages with the aim of taking away the few possessions the forced deportees had left before they reached the city.

Genocide

I was aware of this event, which is still controversial today. Officially, Turkey does not want to recognize this deportation and the many deaths as a genocide. There was great resentment between Erdogan and Germany when the Bundestag officially declared this expulsion of the Armenians from their home to be genocide. So, I asked him whether his family had any private memories of this event and how he had come to still own land there.

Orphans

"Oh, there are still several thousand Armenians there. However, they don't want to be recognized as such. They wear Turkish clothing and there aren't even any Christian churches there anymore. There is nothing to distinguish them from the Muslims. They are the descendants of Armenian orphans adopted by Turkish families. And there are thousands of them, which is a little-known fact. My grandfather was one of them. He was ten years old when both of his parents died in 1915. Today, anyone wishing to have a career has to move to Istanbul like me and take on a Turkish name."

Erika

He became quite personal with these family memories. Just a week before, he had become a first-time father, despite already being 60 years old. He had given the girl a German name: Erika. It went very well with the last name – Erika Kaya. He was so moved that he wanted to give me a golden necklace so that I could share in his joy, even regardless of whether I bought the diamond or not. The eager sales advisor from Reutlingen then brought a heavy necklace over, adorned with gems. The official price was €3,000. Naturally, I could not accept it.

Invitation

He laughed, "The Germans are so married to their principles. They can't even accept a gift. This is my gift to you. Come to stay at my country estate, at the foot of Mount Ararat. I'll show you that you can enjoy life. I bet you have spent your life saving money and are leaving behind a lot of assets without ever having treated yourself. The only sin that you can truly commit in this life is to leave money behind that you haven't spent. All that means is that it was and is completely useless."

Business Sense

Of course, I saw through his arguments and reciprocated with a laugh: "I've heard that the Armenians are more than just proficient businesspeople." Also laughing, he confirmed, "It's true, an Armenian gets this business sense with every Jew he catches. I've got ten Jews bagged." And I believed him, without noticing that he was about to do the same to me.

Why not?

"You like the solitaire. And you have the money for it. So why are you not buying it?"
Well, that wasn't entirely true. Just before, I had bought a silk rug, which had actually also been over my budget. At the moment, I didn't currently have the money for that in cash. In actual fact, I was annoyed at having to justify myself because I didn't want to buy the ring. Dr. Kaya's pushiness was actually shameless.

Telephone Calls with Antwerp

"Wait a moment, I have to speak to the diamond cutters. The diamond is numbered there so they'll be able to tell me by how much I can reduce the price. He went into a side room to make a phone call. "You can save yourself the effort, I'm not going to buy this ring."

Mrs. Ayla

Mrs. Ayla stepped in. The customer advisor. At the time, however, she had a different name which I no longer remember.

"Think about it, it is the most secure way to invest your money. Our monetary system will go bankrupt sooner or later anyway. But the value of diamonds, more than that of gold, remains the most stable. Such a small stone can also be easily hidden. Many a Jew that survived the concentration camps were able to save their most expensive diamonds by swallowing them and afterwards, 'rinsing them out'."

Half Price

Dr. Kaya returned. He was beaming.

"Antwerp has agreed to offer you the ring for half the price, so just €36,000 instead of €72,000."

People say you're supposed to haggle, with half being a fair amount from the starting offer. However, I didn't agree. €36,000 was still too high for me.

"Good! Shake my hand! I am making the worst deal of my life. €30,000 and the stone is yours."

Unlimited

My Mastercard and TUI Card were each limited to €5,000, following the advice of my personal advisor at the KSK Bank. "If you lose the credit cards or they are stolen then at least this way, the damage is limited."

The year before, I had charged my credit cards with €18,000 in the same jewelry shop. That was joined by €1,000 in the leather shop and €1,000 for a rug. My honest bank advisor probably wanted to stop me spending money so carelessly again. However, he put it more subtly.

Instalment Payment

Since the rug I had just bought had had to be paid in full when ordering, I knew that I was still missing €20,000 at any rate. And getting into debt for a stone that I didn't even want to buy was completely out of the question. So, Dr. Kaya made a suggestion. "You also have a monthly income. If you pay ten instalments of €2,000 each, then the solitaire will be paid for."
He fetched an expensive watch, apparently worth €2,000, that I didn't even want. Online research told me I could get it for €500 there.

Mark of Confidence

As a special mark of his confidence, he gave me the details of his private account at a Swiss bank. This unusual transaction could not, of course, take place officially through the jewelry center, but would rather have to be dealt with entirely privately. He gave me the following as his account number: BIC RAIFCH22B77 RAIFFEISEN SCHWEIZ GENOSSEN, IBAN CH9181177000002424222, Payment Recipient: ReMaSe AG Luzern (those were the companies that belonged to him), Reference: 14 Z MO 5595.

I looked at the solitaire again – it was really beyond beautiful – and then made the stupidest mistake of my life.

Visit to the Restaurant

As in the previous year, I was driven to a very elegant restaurant again by a chauffeur. This was situated directly by the sea, separated from the beach only by the shore promenade. A garden with exotic plants drew guests to eat outside in the late summer temperatures. Dr. Kaya excused himself as he still had so many appointments. But he sent a beautiful young Turkish woman to accompany me and I had a wonderful time talking to her.

Financial Recovery

Four and a half years have now passed since then. The stupid mistake was paid off after ten instalments. It even outweighed the joy of having this beautiful diamond. My finances have since recovered from the purchase. What's more, even my girlfriend liked it, unlike in the case with the four rings the previous year, none of which she had liked. I told her that a solitaire was the traditional engagement ring of the aristocracy. But she knew that already, she was from a jeweler's family after all. At that point, we had both been living together for 20 years and were not married. I put the ring on her finger so that now, we were at least engaged. It was our engagement ring. She was beaming. It was one of the last happy memories we had together. She died not long afterwards.

April 1st, 2019

On April 1st of this year, a surprise came out of the blue. Like being hit by a bolt of lightning, I received a huge shock. It was as if it was a very particular kind of April Fool's joke. Dr. Kaya from the D Jewels jewelry center in Antalya called me.

"You have to bail me out. We had a police raid and they even searched through our old order books. I was unable to produce any customs document for your solitaire with the diamond and I am now being fined €300,000. The worst thing is, six other similar cases have been discovered."

Customs Office

He continued, "Luckily I was able to work out a solution with the German customs branch office here in Antalya. Two cases have already almost been solved in this way. The charge will be dropped if you explain that you didn't have the jewelry with you when you traveled back. Secondly, that you did not pay for it until after and thirdly, that while you looked at it when you visited us, you did not order it until later. From Germany."

My Reaction

It was immediately clear to me that Dr. Kaya had avoided the customs charges as neither the post service nor the customs office had been involved in the delivery of the small parcel. A private courier had apparently travelled to Antwerp specially to reach me in Oberndorf and deliver the solitaire personally. I had been informed of his arrival by phone and he also rang my doorbell punctually at the stated time.

Signature

I had had to sign a prepared sheet of paper to confirm that I had received the solitaire and the courier then left. When crossing the border four and a half years ago, I had not had the jewel on me. I would therefore not have been able to produce it. I also paid for it later, excluding the deposit. But the assurance that I had not ordered it until I returned to Germany did not match the facts, nor did I want to confirm that. I did not even see the need to do so.

Customs Officer

"Please call the customs branch office here in Antalya. The customs officer, Mrs. Ayla, a Turkish woman, will be able to give you more information. She wants to rule this in my favor as far as legally possible."

Who is calling who?

I could not fully accept that. That I had to see to Dr. Kaya's customs problems with a Turkish customs officer! She should call me then! But Dr. Kaya assured me that a state office would not be able to legally do that. He would generously reimburse me with any costs, including telephone charges. He begged me to help him. The money for the solitaire that they had given as €26,400 needed to be transacted again so that the customs officer could retain the customs fees from this and then forward the rest to him. Afterwards, the penalty order could be lifted. It would even be enough for just half, that is, €13,200 to be transacted. He had already proven his trust to me when he had delivered the diamond despite ten instalments of €2,000 still being outstanding. I would also have to trust that he would transfer the amount back to me within three days. The sales of his jewelry center amounted to €500 million a year. Surely such an amount would be peanuts to him.

Persistence

I told myself his already rude persistence was just because he was actually in deep trouble and I called the number he had given me. He had given it to me over the phone.
The number was 0090-539 725 69 95.
There, a Mrs. Ayla actually responded, and she was very well-informed. The item was being processed under Case No. 15CK4478.
She assured me that it was true, but that the amount had to change hands again.
The amount of the customs fees would be retained, and the rest forwarded to the company D Jewels.

Email

Meanwhile, I had received an email from Dr. Kaya confirming that the company would transfer the full amount and he specified the account number of the customs office in Turkey. The wording of the email was as follows:

Dear Mr. Landon-Burgher,

The company is obligated to transfer 13,200 EUR + 300 EUR (the additional 300 EUR are for the telephone expenses) back to the account of Mr. Landon-Burgher on Friday 04/05/2019.

Kind regards,

Dr. Ates Kaya
General Director

The following information was given for the transfer:

Recipient:
First Name: SONER
Last Name: AYKUT
Bank Name: YAPI KREDI BANK
IBAN: TR45 0006 7010 0000 0056 9953 24
BIC: YAPITRISXXX
Address: Ege Str. 7-11 DENIZLI TURKEI
Fax No: 0090 212 551 35 71
Tel No: 0090 539 725 70 13

Money Transfer

It all really looked like a scam, similar to the primitive pattern of the "long-lost relative" trick. But I just could not imagine that such an internationally significant jewelry center like D Jewels Antalya would not be serious. And if so, then the fraudster called Dr. Kaya could easily be identified. He was, if not the sole owner, at least a high-ranking employee in the jewelry center. He had had the device that had allowed him to charge €5,000 to my Mastercard and TUI Card each for the deposit. That showed that he had a high position of trust in the company.

Confirmation of Money Received

A call from the customs officer confirmed to me that the amount of €13,200 had been received. She was, however, bound by the regulations, so the entire amount would have to be sent. That would be another €13,200, otherwise the first payment would be for nothing. She had also notified Dr. Kaya of this. He had then immediately gone to her at the office and horribly scolded her.

"And I really didn't deserve that," she complained. At the point that she became so sentimental, I recognized with certainty the voice with the pleasant Swabian accent from the city of Reutlingen again. It was the customer advisor from back then, when she had introduced Dr. Kaya to me as the owner of the jewelry center. So, it was a put-up job by both of them, just like before.

Complaint

I didn't need to wait until the Friday when the money was supposed to be transferred back to my account. This was fraud, but in such a crude form that I could never have considered it possible. I immediately filed criminal charges. But that was far from easy. Who would I report? Dr. Kaya, as well as the name Ayla were surely just cover names. And what exactly was the address of the jewelry center in Antalya?

Turkish Police

What's more, as the German criminal authorities all assured me, the Turkish police pocketed such high bribes from the fraudulent sales centers that they would immediately shelve a complaint from Germany and under no circumstances, open up an investigation.

Mistrust

I then began to have doubts. If this "Dr. Kaya" who had sold me a solitaire for €30,000 resorted to such cheap tricks, then the purchase back then would also have to be treated with caution. Even upon its delivery back then, I had been very unsettled to see that this expensive stone had not come with any kind of certificate and no expertise to confirm the degree of purity, quality of the cut and number of carats.

Expert Opinion

I showed the diamond to a specialist, who told me that it was a very beautiful stone of three carats. Its value was therefore €3,000. With a high level of purity and an excellent cut, the price could be even higher. However, in any case, a certificate was needed.

Silk Rug

A second thing occurred to me. This Dr. Kaya had stated in his email:
Dr. Ates Kaya
Carpet Center
General Director

And as his email address: Sentez Tourism Carpet A.S.

But he worked in the jewelry center! We hadn't talked about the fact that I had just bought a rug at the carpet center before I was driven to the jewelry center with our group. He may have known nothing about it, but clearly, that was not the case.

Arrangements

It then occurred to me that the carpet center and the jewelry center must be exchanging information. There was, in fact, one curious parallel. At the carpet center, I had been shown the most expensive rug straight away, only me. I had been chosen while the others had been spread across other rooms in groups. The cost of the rug was €72,000. It was a Hereke, a silk carpet, silk on silk, so beautiful that it left me speechless. I then bought it for €30,000. The first price I had been given for the diamond was also €72,000. I then lost my nerve at €30,000 again. The jewelry center had therefore been informed of my absolute limit.

Delivery of the Rug

The rug was also not delivered by the customs office, but rather a young man claiming that he had travelled directly from Prague. The photo taken of me when I decided on the rug, so that I would recognize the rug's pattern to see that it was actually the one that I had chosen, was missing. The seal with the dimensions of the rug that had been fixed to it was also missing, just like the label. An unstamped seal had been handed over separately in a plastic bag and the dimensions of the rug had been placed on a small fabric cloth.

Worldwide Looms

At the carpet center, I had been told that this rug had not been knotted in Hereke, as there were no longer any carpet looms there, but rather the workshops had been outsourced to another part of Turkey, where the same techniques and traditional patterns had been incorporated. Even the carpet knotter had been fetched and had worked a full four years on the four million knots. While I could see through that as a sales trick, it was really a silk rug with old Turkish patterns. I knew that much.

Disappointment

But here too I was cheated. On the Certificate of Guarantee, it states "crafted in our company's worldwide looms". The following is given as the origin: D.T.IPEK Ref. Number SH-6875 Only the size is correct 2.4 x 1.66 = 3.98 m²

Material: silk on silk. But that means artificial silk on artificial silk.
Therefore, this too had been a total letdown. The rug had probably been knotted in China. It was definitely not the rug that I had stood on. It had a completely different pattern, a more modern, not traditionally Turkish one, with only the color scheme being as expected.

Price

In China, there is a place that the Chinese, as clever as they are, have called Hereke. They can therefore call the rugs they knot there Hereke. However, not Hereke in Turkey, but Hereke in China. The rugs made there are unusually beautiful. The Chinese are a very skillful people. But the rugs are not made from natural silk, but rather from chemical fibers. I searched online for the price of this kind of rug but was unable to find any information.

Complete and Utter Disaster

I then also got the four rings that I had previously bought for €18,000 on the Cappadocia trip out of my safe. There too, I could now see that I had been scammed. The pre-printed Certificates of Guarantee stated information on the carat of the gold and the carat of the stones. There had also been a guarantee that D Jewels would exchange the goods within five years for others of equal value. After reading the back of the certificate more closely, however, I noticed that the security numbers that had to be stated with any contact with the company were missing. Neither was there any address or telephone number I could use to get in touch with the center.

The price of the jewelry was not indicated anywhere. Upon closer inspection of the rings, I noticed that they did not have an "18 carat" gold stamp anywhere. The emeralds were obviously just colored glass.

What now?

Should I write to D Jewels Antalya and inform them that fraudulent employees are obviously conducting business for their own benefit without the company knowing?
I found a lawyer that exclusively represents charges by cheated customers of this jewelry center online. The main accusation: overpriced goods.

RSD Travel Service

Should I tell this travel agency that they are taking their customers to fraudulent shopping centers? I am now convinced that they are running a joint operation with these sales centers for leather goods, rugs and jewelry, and that they pocket commission whenever they take a customer there that can be ripped off.

The Only Solution

All travelers who have ever flown with RSD Travel Service and perhaps purchased something should check whether the quality of their purchases matches the price. Possibly, they did not realize that they had been scammed until later, like me. If future travelers with RSD are more careful when shopping, the sales centers will no longer be able to charge such high premiums per shopper. The "free coffee trips through the air" will become rarer. If a 14-day round trip to Morocco or Turkey and a relaxing holiday in a 4-star hotel for €199 no longer bring in a profit, these trips are sure to be stopped completely.

Class Action Lawsuit

Perhaps all those affected could even join forces and prepare a class action lawsuit. Maybe then it would be possible to force the Turkish police or even Interpol to open up an investigation.